Little, Brown and Company

Hachette Book Group
237 Park Avenue, New York, NY 10017
Visit our website at lb-kids.com

LB kids is an imprint of Little, Brown and Company.
The LB kids name and logo are trademarks of Hachette Book Group, Inc.

The publisher is not responsible for websites (or their content) that are not owned by the publisher.

First Edition: June 2014

Library of Congress Cataloging-in-Publication Data

Sazaklis, John.
    Return of the dino bot / adapted by John Sazaklis ; based on the episode
"Return of the Dino Bot" by Luke McMullen. — First edition.
        pages cm
    "Transformers Rescue Bots."
    ISBN 978-0-316-18867-8 (pbk)
    I. McMullen, Luke. II. Transformers, Rescue Bots (Television program)
III. Title.
    PZ7.S27587Re 2014
    [E]—dc23

                                                                2013029903

10 9 8 7 6 5 4 3 2

CW

Printed in the United States of America

Licensed By:

TRANSFORMERS RESCUE BOTS

Return of the Dino Bot

Adapted by John Sazaklis
Based on the episode "Return of the Dino Bot"
written by Luke McMullen

LITTLE, BROWN & COMPANY
LB kids

Before Cody started patrol, his phone rang.

"Griffin Rock Emergency," he answered. "A dinosaur? Lurking around Griffin Rock Lab? We're on it."

Cody saw the Rescue Bots exchange surprised looks. "Sometimes fog can make you see things that aren't really there," he explained. "No harm in checking it out."

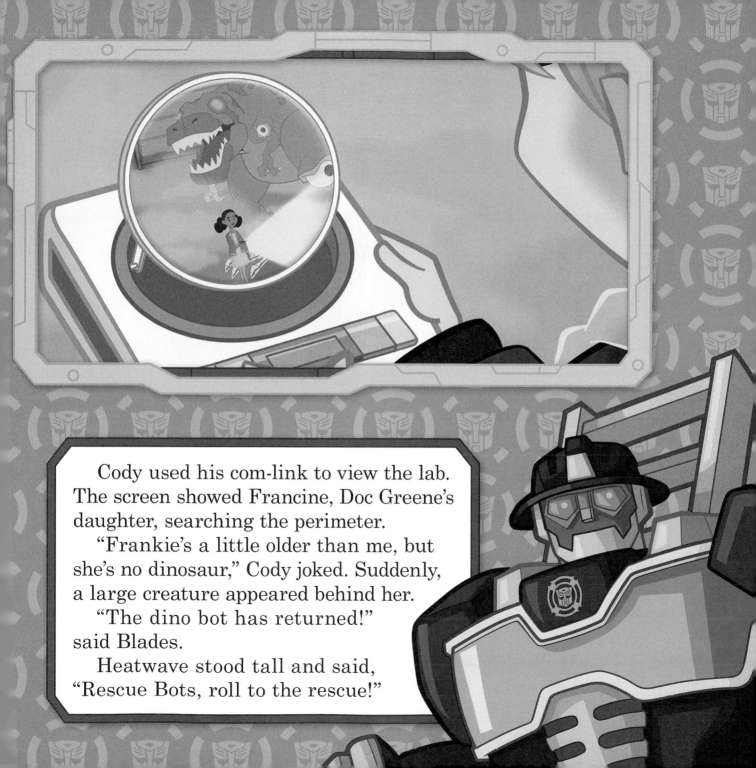

Cody used his com-link to view the lab. The screen showed Francine, Doc Greene's daughter, searching the perimeter.

"Frankie's a little older than me, but she's no dinosaur," Cody joked. Suddenly, a large creature appeared behind her.

"The dino bot has returned!" said Blades.

Heatwave stood tall and said, "Rescue Bots, roll to the rescue!"

The robots switched into vehicle mode and rushed to Griffin Rock Lab. Cody and his sister, Dani, hitched a ride inside Blades.

"The dino bot was supposed to be shut down and in the museum," Dani said. "Are you sure that's what you saw?"

"Yes, and it was stalking Frankie!" replied Cody. "Look, there they are!"

Blades landed near his teammates Boulder, Heatwave, and Chase. They all changed forms and surrounded the mechanical menace.

"Attention, human! Take cover!" Heatwave said to Frankie. He aimed his water blasters at the dino bot and prepared to fire.

Frankie ran between Heatwave and the dino bot. "Wait!" she cried, waving her arms. "He's friendly now. His name is Trex!"

Heatwave lowered his blasters. He and the other Rescue Bots were confused.

"That's right," Doc Greene said. "I've reprogrammed the dino bot to protect our lab. The other day, an intruder tried to break into our computer system."

"Yikes!" replied Graham, one of Cody's brothers. "A hacker could control everything automated in town!"

Suddenly, an alarm blared. "Security breach!" Trex announced. "Threat: maximum!"

"Oh no!" Doc Greene shouted.

The friends gathered around a large monitor. There was chaos in the city. The Rescue Bots changed into vehicles again and zoomed off.

Meanwhile, the automated devices in Griffin Rock had gone haywire—even the fire hydrants. They shot water at the Rescue Bots. "Every piece of tech controlled by the city's mainframe has gone berserk!" Heatwave cried.

Before the Bots could get their bearings, an out-of-control lawn mower charged at them. Its sharp, shiny blades were spinning and heading straight for Cody!

Boulder and Chase whisked their young friend out of harm's way.

"Well, that was a close shave!" Boulder said.

At the lab, Doc Greene and Frankie discovered that the cause of the chaos was a computer virus. It had reprogrammed the dino bot from harmless guard dog to predator. Trex's first instruction was to destroy the humans!

"We must plug my laptop into the mainframe," Doc Greene said as they ran from Trex. "It's the only computer not affected."

Thinking quickly, Doc Greene lured the dino bot to the other side of the lab. This gave Frankie time to upload the software needed to remove the virus.

Before the upload was complete, Trex screeched and ran out of the lab, disappearing into the fog.

87%

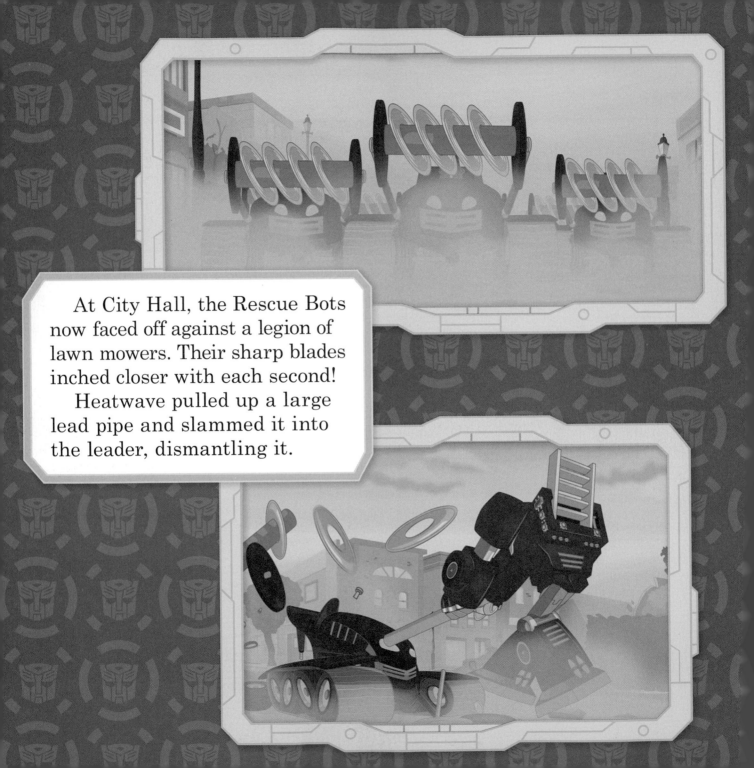

At City Hall, the Rescue Bots now faced off against a legion of lawn mowers. Their sharp blades inched closer with each second!

Heatwave pulled up a large lead pipe and slammed it into the leader, dismantling it.

"Brilliant idea, boss," Chase shouted. He and Boulder followed Heatwave's example and grabbed pipes of their own.

"Batters up!" cried Boulder.

In no time, the Rescue Bots turned all the lawn mowers into scrap metal.

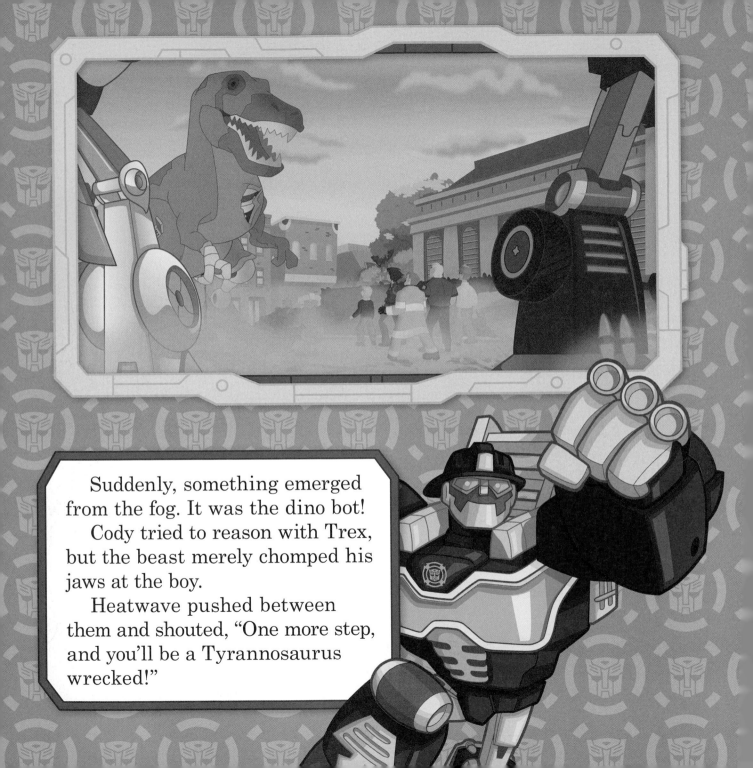

Suddenly, something emerged from the fog. It was the dino bot!

Cody tried to reason with Trex, but the beast merely chomped his jaws at the boy.

Heatwave pushed between them and shouted, "One more step, and you'll be a Tyrannosaurus wrecked!"

The angry dino bot roared at Heatwave and then tore a lamppost from the ground. He charged at the Rescue Bots and nearby civilians.

"Stop that dinosaur!" shouted Chief Burns.

"Rescue Bots, roll to the rescue!" Heatwave commanded.

The robots rushed toward Trex as he threw the lamppost at them. Boulder caught the flying post. Then he tossed it back at the dino bot.

Heatwave attacked Trex with his water blasters. Disoriented, the creature spun in circles and swatted Heatwave with his tail!

In a flash, Blades switched into a helicopter and zoomed toward Trex. He zipped around the dino bot's head.

While the beast was distracted, Boulder shot a wire cable around his foot. Then Boulder zigged and zagged around Trex, tying the dino bot's legs together.

Unbalanced, Trex fell forward onto the pavement.

Before the dino bot could break free, the Rescue Bots piled onto him like a Bot rugby team. Trex wasn't going anywhere!

Together, the Rescue Bots secured Trex and brought him back to the lab. Doc Greene completely removed the virus from the dino bot.

"Trex is a good boy now," said the scientist. The friends were relieved that life was going to go back to normal.

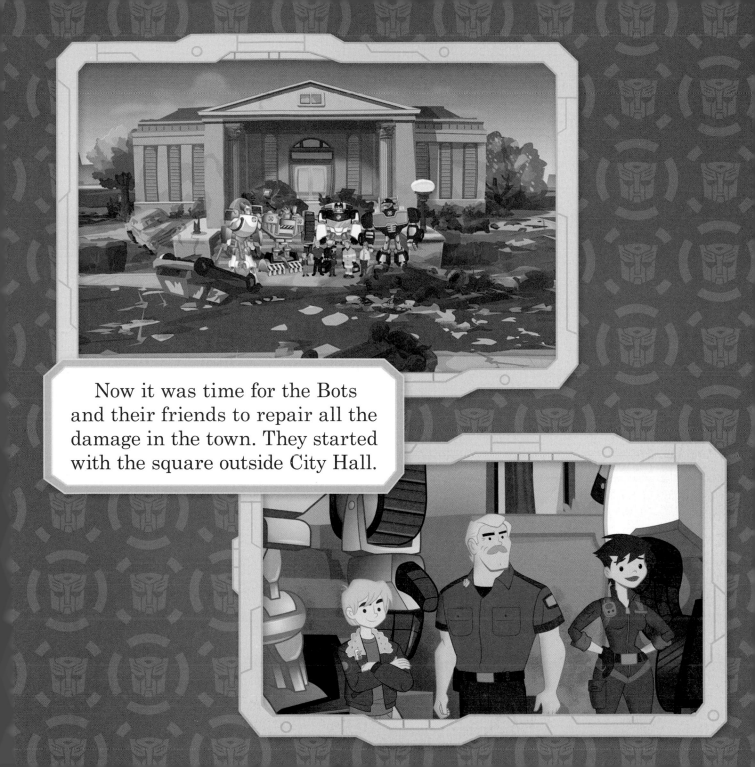

Now it was time for the Bots and their friends to repair all the damage in the town. They started with the square outside City Hall.

"Let us combine our efforts and bring Griffin Rock back to its former glory," Heatwave said. "That's what we do," Blades replied. "We're the Rescue Bots!"